To Charlie

From...........

It was Christmas Eve and Charlie
was snug and warm in his cosy bed.
He was trying so hard to go to sleep,
but he could hear strange noises.

It wasn't the sound of sleigh bells.
It wasn't the sound of reindeer hoofs on the roof.
It wasn't even the sound of Santa unpacking his sack.

It was more of a

HARRUMPH!

and an

OOF!

It was no use.

There would be no sleep for Charlie
until he had found out what
was making that noise.

Charlie crept down the stairs
and peered into the living room.
There were three stockings
hanging from the fireplace.

One of them belonged to Charlie. But where had the other two come from? Suddenly, a muffled voice came from the chimney.

Charlie

"Oh, dear. I'm even **more** stuck now!"

There was a scuffling sound from behind the Christmas tree, and Charlie jumped when a small elf appeared.

Charlie

"Uh, hello," said the elf. "I guess you've caught us!"

Charlie listened as the elf explained
that Santa was stuck in the chimney.
The elf had tried to pull him out, but the
only things that had come down so far
were Santa's boots and trousers!

"I can help you," suggested Charlie.
"I'll hold Santa's feet and we can both pull."
The elf agreed. "Between us we might
be able to get him unstuck."

Charlie firmly grasped both of Santa's feet.
Suddenly a light went on upstairs.
"Charlie, is that you?" called his mum.
"Back to bed now, please, or Santa won't come!"

Charlie

At that moment Santa shot back up the chimney... with Charlie still hanging onto his feet!

The poor elf could not believe his eyes.
But there was no time to think...
Charlie's mum was coming
out of her bedroom.

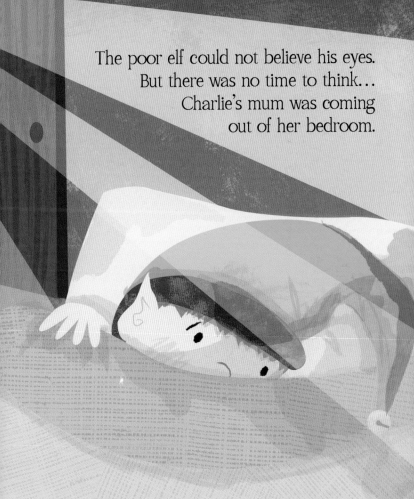

"I'm coming!" squeaked the elf. He hurried
up the stairs and jumped into Charlie's
bed, pulling the covers over his head.
"Night night, sweetie," said Charlie's mum.

Meanwhile, up on the roof, Santa and Charlie had landed in a heap. The clever reindeer had hooked their reins under Santa's arms and pulled as hard as they could.

"Good work!" said Santa, brushing himself off. "No more mince pies for me tonight!"

Charlie scrambled to his feet, but Santa
was so busy that he didn't notice Charlie
and the elf had switched places!

"I think we had better deliver the rest
of the presents first," said Santa,
"and leave this house for last."

Santa climbed into the driver's seat.

"Elf, you get the presents ready for our next destination," he called over his shoulder.
"But I'm not Elf..." replied Charlie.

Santa wasn't listening.
He was talking to the reindeer.
"Up, up and away!" Santa called,
and the reindeer took off before
Charlie had time to explain.

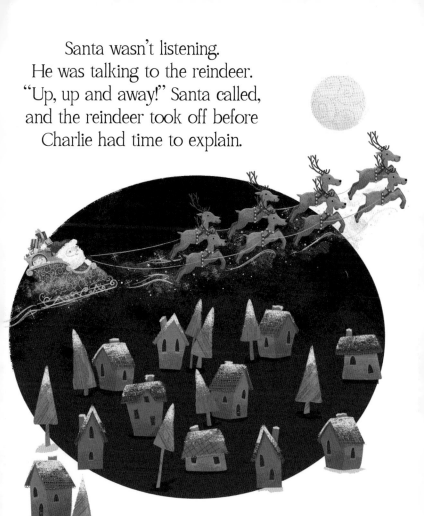

Charlie held on tight as the sleigh
soared high over the rooftops
and into the night sky.

Surrounded by sacks, Charlie was
so busy working out which presents were
which that there was no time to let Santa
know a mistake had been made.

There were **big**
presents for the cities,

and **SHINY** presents
for the towns.

There were **ODD**-shaped
presents for the villages,

and **unusual**
presents for the farms.

To
Charlie

As they landed at their next stop, Santa decided that he couldn't risk getting stuck in a chimney again.

"Elf, I think you had better make the deliveries from now on," Santa said. "I'll sort the presents."

Charlie *shimmied* down chimneys.

He **squeezed** through cat flaps.

And, if all else failed, he used Santa's *magic* key to let himself in.

In each house Charlie picked up the mince pies to take to Mrs Claus and carrots for the reindeer.

Finally there was just one sack left, and
Santa still hadn't realised his mistake!
The sleigh headed back over the
rooftops to Charlie's house.

Sliding down his chimney with
a sack of his own presents was
the most fun Charlie had ever had.

He put his presents under the
Christmas tree, then picked up
Santa's trousers and boots and
placed them in the sack.

Charlie

To
Charlie

"Psst! Elf, where are you?" whispered Charlie.

A very happy Elf appeared, rubbing his eyes. "I've had such a nice nap," he said. Charlie handed over the sack and waved as Elf disappeared up the chimney.

Back in his cosy bed, Charlie could
hear the sounds of jingling sleigh bells,
reindeer hoofs on the roof and, very faintly,

"Ho, ho, ho!

Merry Christmas!"

Or was that,

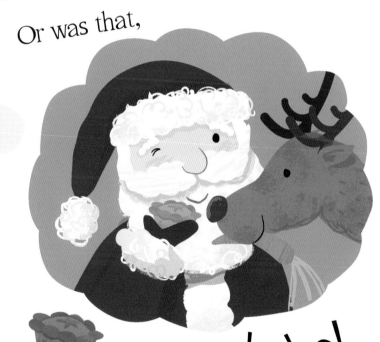

"Ho, ho, ho!
Yummy mince pies!"?

Write your name on the labels.

Draw yourself as an elf.

Written by Katherine Sully
Illustrated by Julia Seal
Designed by Nicola Moore

This edition published by HOMETOWN WORLD in 2018
Hometown World Ltd
1 Queen Street
Bath
BA1 1HE

www.hometownworld.co.uk

Follow us @hometownworldbooks

ISBN 978-1-78553-562-8
All rights reserved
Printed in Italy
HTW_PO201814

put me
in the story®

Bestselling books starring your child!
www.putmeinthestory.co.uk